Winnie the Pooh

Is My Shirt Getting Smaller?

Roo hopped out of bed early one morning and put on his favorite shirt. But this morning, something was different. Today, Roo had to tug very hard just to get it over his head. When he did, the shirt seemed tight. "Is my shirt getting smaller?" he wondered.

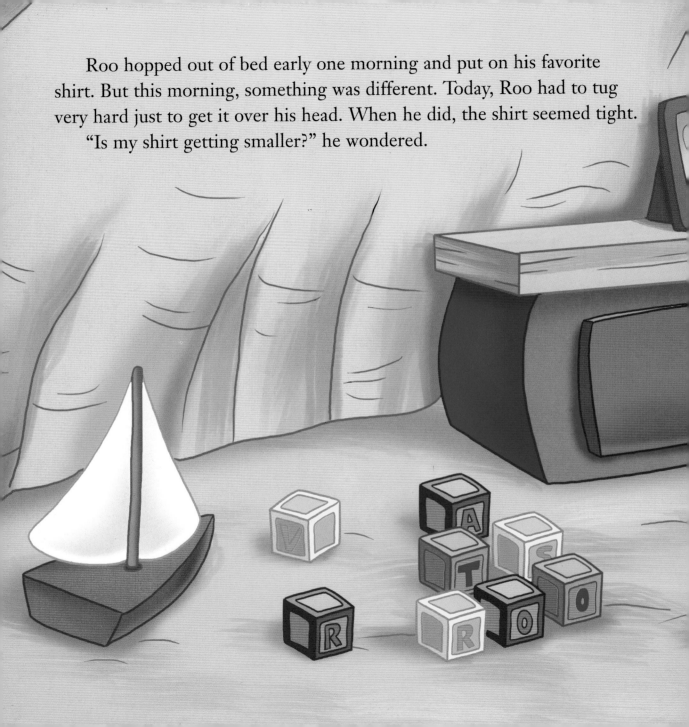

At breakfast, Roo sat in the same chair he sat in every day. But this time, Roo's feet almost touched the floor.

"I don't think this has ever happened before," thought Roo. "Oh, no! Is my chair getting smaller, too?"

"Here's your oatmeal," said Kanga, handing Roo his favorite bowl.
Roo ate it all, but he wanted more.
"That must have been a smaller bowl than I usually have," he thought.

"Mama," Roo said, "everything in our house is shrinking!"

"Really?" Kanga said with a smile. "What makes you think so, dear?"

"Well," said Roo, "this morning my shirt got smaller. And when I sat down, my feet could almost touch the floor. And look!" Roo held up his empty bowl. "I ate up all my oatmeal, which I never do. My bowl must have gotten smaller, too."

"Hmmm," Kanga said thoughtfully. "I wonder what's happening."

Before Kanga had a chance to explain, Tigger came bouncing through the door.

"Hoo-hoo-hoo, Buddy Boy," called Tigger. "And good morning to you, Mrs. Kanga."

"Tigger, Tigger!" cried Roo, jumping up and down. "Our house is shrinking!"

"You don't say!" said Tigger. "That would be something!"

"What if everything in the Wood is getting smaller?" asked Roo.

"We'd better go innervestigate," said Tigger as he and Roo bounced out the door.

Their first stop was the Sandy Pit. Roo hopped across it. Then he turned to Tigger and said, "It took me only three hops to get across. It used to take me five. The Sandy Pit must be shrinking!"

"Whaddya know! The Wood is getting smaller! Yipperee!" shouted Tigger. Then, for once, Tigger paused to think. "At least I think yipperee."

"Let's go tell everyone," said Roo, leading Tigger toward Owl's house.

"Owl, Owl!" Roo called out. But there was no answer. Tigger and Roo climbed up anyway.

Owl wasn't home, but his friends saw a note pinned to his door.

"There he is!" cried Tigger. "Over in that tree. Come here, Little Buddy, and I'll carry you down."

"I can get down by myself," said Roo. Then Roo's eyes got big and round. "But I never could before. Owl's tree must be shrinking!"

"Owl!" Roo cried from down below. "We have something to tell you."

Owl flew down to greet his friends. "I hope it's good news on this wonderful morning. You see, my little friends have finally grown big and strong enough to fly. And I'm teaching them how!"

Then Owl turned and called out as loudly as he could, "Everyone fly on the count of three. One...two...three!" Suddenly, the air was filled with little birds, swooping and soaring along.

"Very good," called Owl. Then he turned to Tigger and Roo. "Now, what is it you wanted to tell me?"

"Your house is shrinking. The Sandy Pit is shrinking. The Wood is shrinking!" said Roo, hopping up and down.

"Ridickilous, but true," said Tigger.

"Oh, dear," said Owl. Then he called to his little friends. "Everyone practice flying home. Lessons are over for the day!"

"Let's go see if Pooh looks the same," said Tigger. "He might be shrinking, too."

They knocked on Pooh's door, but no one answered. Then Tigger looked inside and said, "Nobody's home."

"Let me see," said Roo, looking in the window. "Oh, no! I could never reach the window before. Pooh's house is shrinking! We've got to find him and tell him!"

"Hello there," called Pooh as he and Piglet walked up the path. "Looking for someone?"

"You, Pooh Boy," said Tigger. "We've come to tell you something important."

"Everything is shrinking!" cried Roo. "First my shirt got smaller. Then my chair got so little my feet could almost touch the floor."

"And Roo only needed three hops to cross the Sandy Pit instead of five," said Tigger.

"Oh, dear," said Pooh. "We'd better go and see if my Thinking Spot is shrinking, too."

On the way to Pooh's Thinking Spot, the friends stopped at the pond.

Then Tigger called out to ducklings that were gliding by behind their mother.

"Hello there, ducklings! When you grow up to be the same size as your mom, let's all go for a swim."

"Bother," said Pooh as he sat down in his Thinking Spot. "If everything in the Hundred-Acre Wood is getting smaller, maybe the ducklings will always be ducklings."

Seeing the ducklings gave Owl an idea.

"Roo," said Owl, "I think we need to visit the climbing tree."

As the friends gathered by their favorite place to swing, Owl told Roo to reach up and grab onto the lowest branch. Roo began to swing from the branch. Everyone smiled and nodded. "Well, I'll be daffodilled!" cried Tigger.

"What? What?" asked Roo, hopping up and down.

"Roo," Owl began, "remember when you were so small you couldn't reach that branch even when you hopped your highest and held your arms straight up?"

"Now you can swing with no problem," said Piglet.

"So the Wood isn't shrinking, Roo," said Pooh. "And your shirt isn't getting smaller. It's just that you're..."

"...getting bigger!" cried Roo. "Hooray for me!"

Growing Up

Just like Roo, from the time humans and animals are born, they are always changing and growing. But like the ducks, the birds, and Roo, there are steps to take to be sure you grow up in the healthiest way possible.

1) Like ducklings, drink plenty of water.

2) Be sure to eat lots of vegetables and fruits.

3) Like birds, eat lots of protein. Birds eat lots of insects and worms. You can stick to yogurt, cheese, chicken, fish, and meat.

4) Like all animals, get plenty of sunshine and exercise.

5) And get lots of sleep!

Young children love to observe, discuss and compare. Here's an activity that will help them do just that:

Step 1: You'll need four feet of paper and a ruler. Mark off two, three, and four feet with the ruler and fill in the inches in between.

Step 2: Tape your growth chart to a wall.

Step 3: Measure your preschooler and mark it on the chart.

Step 4: Revisit the chart every few weeks to measure any growth.